For Elizabeth and Catherine

Printed in Italy.

First U.S. Edition 1986
12345678910

Library of Congress Cataloging in Publication Data
Ormerod, Jan.
Just like me.
Summary: Even though her baby brother is bald like
an egg and moves like a puppy, a little girl decides
that he is really just like her.
[1. Babies - Fiction.   2. Brothers and sisters - Fiction]   I. Title.
PZ7.0634Ju   1986   [E]   85-18056
ISBN 0-688-04211-2

Just Like Me

Jan Ormerod

LOTHROP, LEE & SHEPARD BOOKS
NEW YORK

Granny says my brother is just like me.

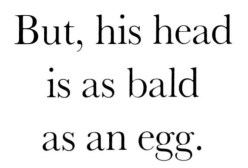

But, his head
is as bald
as an egg.

His ears
are as pink
as a rabbit's.

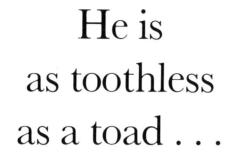

He is
as toothless
as a toad . . .

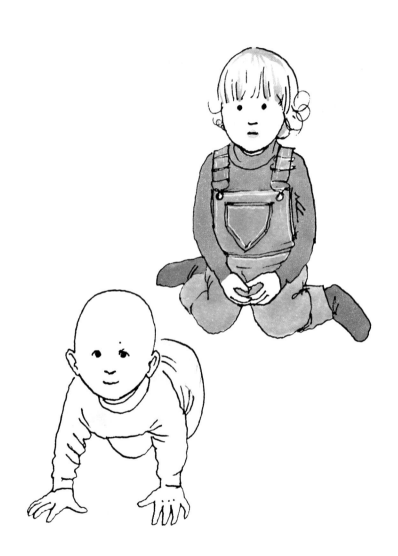

and he goes about
on all-fours,
like a puppy.

My baby brother
eats like
a little pig . . .

and he's too
little to sit
on the potty.

Granny says,

when I was a baby,

I was bald as an ⬭ ,

had pink ears like a 🐰 ,

was toothless as a 🐸 ,

crawled like a 🐕 ,

and ate like a 🐖 .